TOO MANY MONSTERS!

Written and Illustrated by Ann Garrison Greenleaf

Derrydale Books

New York · Avenel, New Jersey

One Halloween night on Hawthorne Street,
Kelly waved her wand, closed her eyes, and made
a wish. And when she opened her eyes...

...her room still wasn't clean. So she kicked everything under the bed.

"Knock, knock!" Kelly's father poked his head into her bedroom. "All set, princess? Doesn't it feel great to have a clean room?" her father asked. He looked around the room, smiling until he came to the bed. "Just a minute, young lady."

"What's all this! Goodness gracious!" He began to pull things out—a half-eaten apple, half a baloney sandwich, a can of fruit juice....

"I didn't put those there!" Kelly was as surprised as her father.

He looked at her sternly. "You've had all day to straighten up in here," he said. "For Heaven's sake, Kelly! I can't even imagine what might be under there! Well, this could be your greatest Halloween adventure ever."

He put a helmet on her head and handed her a popgun and a flashlight. "Kelly the Explorer! Be brave. Be cautious. If you haven't returned in an hour, we'll send in a rescue party." He shook her hand and left.

"Phooey." Kelly frowned.

Kelly pulled up her comforter and yelled into
the darkness, "I'm coming in!" She took a deep
breath and mumbled to herself, "I'm not afraid!"

As soon as she crawled under the bed, Kelly heard a whimper. She froze, then stammered, "Who's there?"

The whites of two huge eyes blinked at her. "Don't shoot!"

Kelly turned on her flashlight.

"You shouldn't point guns at people," the monster said.
"Shame on you!"

Kelly put the gun down. "It's just a toy."

"Doesn't matter," said the monster. "You could poke somebody's eye out." He began to clean his claws with a coat hanger. "What are you doing here, anyway?"

"What am *I* doing here?" Kelly yelled. "What are *you* doing here? This is *my* bed!"

"But you've never even been under here before," the monster pointed out.

Kelly put her hands on her hips. "Well, I'm here now!"

"Why?"

"I have to clean my room," Kelly moaned.

The monster began combing his hair with a bamboo rake. "It's about time," he said. "This place is a pigsty. Do you have *any* idea how hard it is for me to keep some kind of order with you kicking junk under here willy-nilly?"

"Me!" Kelly shouted. "What about the baloney sandwich? That's not mine!"

The monster blushed. "I didn't think you'd notice."

Kelly sighed. "Oh, it doesn't matter. I'll never get done in time to trick or treat anyway."

The monster scratched his head. "Look," he said, "I don't get out much. If you take me with you, I'll help you clean up this mess."

"Deal!" Kelly agreed. "You start with that pile!"

Just when they put everything in one big pile
in the center of the room, they heard a knock at
the door. "Quick!" Kelly whispered. "The closet!"
As fast as they could, they scooped up the
entire pile and stuffed it in Kelly's closet.

Kelly's father opened the door a crack. "I've organized a search party, Kelly. We'll find you if we have to travel to the four corners of the earth. Wait! What's this? A snake behind the door! A clue, men!"

Kelly giggled.

"Hark!" her father yelled. "Can it be? Kelly has returned!" He rushed over to hug her and noticed the monster. "And with a friend. Welcome."

"Can we *please* go now, Dad?" the ghost said.

"Yes, yes, we're off! Nice costume," Kelly's father told the monster.

When they got home late that night, Kelly went straight to bed.

"Good night," she said.

"Sweet dreams," said the monster.

Kelly had just fallen asleep when she felt a thump from below.

"What?" she cried, sitting up.

"Are you awake?" asked the monster.

"Of course I'm awake," she growled. "You kicked my bed."

"I can't sleep," said the monster.

"Read a book," Kelly said, putting her head down on the pillow. She heard a long sigh. And then another.

"Oh, honestly," Kelly sat up, turning on the light. "What *is* the matter?"

"I need my blanket," the monster whined. "It's in the closet, with everything else."

Kelly rolled her eyes. "OK, but we'd better be careful. Opening that door could be dangerous."

They tiptoed to the closet and Kelly gently turned the door knob...

"Watch out!" The closet's contents poured
out in a rush.

"Phew!" Kelly and the monster said. Then
they picked themselves up and began to look
through the pile.

"What does your blanket look like?" Kelly
asked.

"It's blue and white with satin trim," said the monster. He peeked into the closet. "There it is! You take one end and I'll take the other. One, two, three, pull!"

"Yikes!" A new monster tumbled out of the
closet, landed with a thud and looked around.

"Well," he said, "you two sure took your
time! I've been trapped in there for hours. You
going to eat that? I'm starved." He grabbed a
popcorn ball and headed for the bed. "You might as
well wait 'til morning to clean up that junk—it's a
jungle in there. By the way, is there another pillow?
I can't sleep without a pillow."

Kelly sighed. "OK, come on. You can both
share mine. But just for tonight." She pulled the
blanket up and yawned. "Are there any more
monsters in here?" she asked.

**The first monster smiled and closed his
eyes. "I don't know," he said. "When was the last
time you cleaned your toy box?"**